AN UNOFFICIAL GAMER'S QUEST

ESCAPE FROM THE OVERWORLD

DANICA DAVIDSON

Sky Pony Press
New York

Sky Pony Press books may be purchased in bulk at special discounts for sales promotion, corporate gifts, fund-raising, or educational purposes. Special editions can also be created to specifications. For details, contact the Special Sales Department, Sky Pony Press, 307 West 36th Street, 11th Floor, New York, NY 10018 or info@skyhorsepublishing.com.

Sky Pony® is a registered trademark of Skyhorse Publishing, Inc.®, a Delaware corporation.

Visit our website at www.skyponypress.com.

10 9 8 7 6 5 4 3 2 1

Library of Congress Cataloging-in-Publication Data is available on file.

Cover design by Owen Corrigan
Cover artwork by Lordwhitebear

Print ISBN: 978-1-63450-103-3
Ebook ISBN: 978-1-63450-104-0

Printed in Canada

CHAPTER 1

THE MONSTERS CAME OUT WHENEVER IT GOT DARK. I didn't realize the sun was setting until it was too late.

I had gotten totally caught up in what I was doing: building my very first tree house. When you're the son of the man who's the best builder around, it means you have a lot to prove. I was Stevie, from a long line of Steves, in a land where just about everyone was named Steve. Here's the thing, though: my dad is The Steve.

No one calls him that to his face, but everyone knows him, and everyone knows I am his son. My dad had forged a diamond sword when he was twelve, only one year older than I am now. That sword was so good he still uses it to this day to slay zombies, and he is known as the best zombie slayer around.

He has the greatest farm in the area, too, with wheat, pumpkins, carrots, and everything else. He likes to go mining and isn't scared of going down into the fiery realm of

1

the Nether, even though there are even worse monsters there and no sunlight to protect you from them.

And then there's everything Dad has built. The giant farmhouse. The barn. The summer home. The winter home. You get the idea. All the houses had iron doors to keep monsters out, plus torches to keep them from spawning near us. My dad also tamed an ocelot he found, making her into a sweet cat, because cats are good at keeping creepers away.

I would help Dad farm and go with him to the Nether, but when it came to making and handling things on my own, that was different. My dad would brag, "Someday, Stevie is going to be a great builder." But it didn't feel like he was encouraging me or anything. It felt more like he was saying, "Stevie's going to be a great builder because he has no other option except to live in my shadow."

One thing my dad had never built was a tree house, so I decided that would be where I'd have to show off my skills. The first thing I decided to build was my own stone tools. They wouldn't be as cool as a diamond sword, but everyone had to start somewhere.

I picked a tree that was just out of sight from the biggest house Dad had built, which was the house we were living in at the time. I figured this gave me enough distance so that it was *my* tree, but it was still not too far from Dad or home.

Next, I walked all over and gathered wood from oak trees. My dad had a whole stockpile of obsidian sitting around that could be used for building—though I knew better than to touch that. Obsidian was really difficult to get, so I knew Dad wouldn't want me to use it after all the hard work he put into collecting it. Besides, I wanted to show Dad I could do everything on my own. I didn't even buy anything from the village because trading emeralds for supplies would have made it easier for me.

After I'd gotten my handmade supplies together, I went out to the tree and made a ladder out of sticks. The next step was to clear out the leaves in the tree so that there would be room for my tree house. Once I had the space in the tree, I started to set up the blocks for the floor. Block by block, that's how I did it. After the floor was done, I got to work on setting up blocks for the walls. I wasn't a big fan of heights, so I didn't put the house too high into the tree.

As I built the tree house, I had lots of time to think about things. Like how the tree house was turning out okay, even though I'd been really nervous about it. I'd finally jumped from making small items to making something bigger—something so big you could actually live in it.

Maybe I could get some of the kids from the village to come over and hang out with me. Whenever Dad and I went to the village to trade, I would look for the kids my age and we'd play games like putting saddles on pigs and having little pig races. But the kids never came to visit me. It was lonely out here in the country. It would also be great if Dad could hang out in my tree house with me, and for once it would be a home *I* built, not him.

When it started getting difficult to see my work, I realized I'd made a major mistake. One that could be deadly. I spent so much time thinking and building that I wasn't watching the sun. It was slipping down toward the horizon, the sky going gray.

When the sun went away, monsters—or mobs— would spawn. They liked to seek out people, especially ones out in the dark, away from everyone else.

Very quickly I made my way toward the ladder and began to hurry down it.

It's okay, I told myself. I knew Dad would be furious if I got home after dark, but what really mattered was that I would get home. *And I will*, I thought. Just because I couldn't see home didn't mean it wasn't nearby . . . *I'll make it*, I told myself, *I'll make it*.

As soon as I was partway down the ladder, I saw that I wouldn't make it.

CHAPTER 2

ON THE GROUND, JUST A FEW FEET AWAY, STOOD a creeper. Creepers may look harmless with their armless bodies and their frowny faces, but don't let looks fool you: they're some of the most feared mobs in the Overworld because of the way they can silently sneak up on you and because of the scary amount of destruction they can cause.

I was hanging from the ladder, frantically trying to grab some sort of tool out of the pouch I had tied around my waist. I had exactly 1.5 seconds to fight the creeper, or else it would explode.

In my panic, I couldn't even lift the lid of my pouch. But 1.5 seconds gave me enough time to realize how bad this was, try to do something, recognize there wasn't going to be enough time, and open my mouth to shout, "No!" as if a creeper has ever listened to a human.

The little green mob looked up at me, started shaking and shivering, and then everything exploded.

I fell back against the ground with the wind knocked out of me. My pouch flew through the air and landed with a thud somewhere off in the darkness. The creeper was gone, dead. They always die when they explode, and they love to take your work with them. Overhead I could see the floor of my tree house break into pieces.

I lay there, trying to catch my breath. It was full night now, the square moon overhead. I didn't want to admit it, but I wished Dad was around to help me. But then again, I was glad he wasn't, because I didn't want him to see my ruined tree house. Tomorrow I would have to start over on my building. No good creepers!

I struggled to get up but I was too weak. It was going to be a little bit before I'd be able to sit up and limp my way back to the house.

Dad would never give sympathy, even though I could have really used some right then. He'd never had any of his work blown up by a creeper.

I shut my eyes against the square moon and breathed deeply. I needed food and milk to feel better, and then a good night's sleep. I didn't want to think about how much I'd been hurt. I especially didn't want to think about how it was still dark. Or that my tools were off in the distance and I was now weaponless. Or that home was as far away as ever. Instead of all the scary things, I thought about how I would get back to work on my building in the morning. Lots of people in the Overworld have had their hard work blown up thanks to a sneaky creeper, so maybe the next time I went to the village, I would tell the other kids about it and we'd bond and I'd make real friends

And that's when I realized I wasn't alone. In the distance I could hear the zombies moaning.

CHAPTER 3

TWO ZOMBIES LURCHED TOWARD ME, THE MOONLIGHT bringing out the putrid greenness of their skin. I opened my mouth to scream for help, knowing it was the only energy I had left. I couldn't get up. I couldn't run. Out of the darkness another zombie materialized, following the others. More moans came from behind me, but I couldn't move my head enough to witness how many zombies were moving toward me from the back—or how close they were.

I clamped down my eyelids so I didn't have to see the ones right in front of me. But I could hear them approaching. Their gurgling rasps were just over me, their decomposed breath almost touching my body. Then when all seemed lost, I heard someone running as fast as he could. I opened my eyes just in time to see the blue streak of a diamond sword come crashing down on the zombie that was kneeling right over me.

"Get away!" Dad was yelling. "You filthy mobs!"

The zombie fell back and disappeared immediately, so Dad turned to the next closest target.
Undeterred by the weapon, the zombie continued to pitch
forward. Dad finished that mob off with a quick stab of
his sword, and then he turned to face another zombie.
The third zombie was coming at him, its moans loud in
the night, its arms outstretched. It was a scary sight, but
Dad was ready. He was always ready, no matter how bad
the situation was. All I could do was watch helplessly as
the sword arced in the air and took out the zombie.

Three more zombies were approaching from behind.
When I looked straight up I could see them, looming
overhead. They were the ones I'd heard before but couldn't
see since they were moving in from behind.

Now Dad turned to them with a furious look in
his eye. Letting out an angry roar, he charged. All three
zombies lunged for him at once, but one perfect swipe
of his sword took them all out.

The next thing I knew, Dad was sheathing his sword
and coming over to my side.

"Stevie!" he said. "You know better than to be out
at night!"

That was Dad for you. He could never say, "I'm glad
you're alive" or "You're so important to me." He always
had to say a put-down, like, "You know better."

I couldn't really argue with him, though, because he
was right that I did know better. I'd gotten so caught up
in trying to prove myself with the tree house that I had
cut corners when it had come to my own safety.

Dad looked up at the tree house and *tsk-tsked*. "And a creeper," he muttered.

Well, there was no keeping secrets from him. With a huff, Dad hefted me up against him and half dragged me back toward the house.

"I'm glad to see you're taking an interest in building," he was saying as he found my pouch and put it around his own waist. "But there's a point when it's just reckless."

Off in the distance I could hear the moaning hiss of more zombies, but this time none of them got too close to us. Soon we could see our house with its protective iron doors. All the torches were lit out front.

Dad lay me down in my bed and Ossie the cat jumped up next to me to lick my face as her way of helping me feel better. While I lay there, Dad got food and milk from the kitchen.

"Here," he said, sitting me up and helping me eat. He sat next to me on the bed. "You're going to need to get this all down and rest. We'll have to go to the village the day after tomorrow."

We had planned to go to the village the next afternoon for trading, but Dad saw I needed time to rest. I nodded weakly and drank more milk, starting to feel a little better already.

"But the thing is, Stevie," he said, and I knew he was getting to the point of the lecture, "you're eleven years old now. You're going to be a man before long. I went out looking for you at sunset, and you are lucky I went in the right direction. If I hadn't gotten there just in time . . ." He trailed off and shook his head, not wanting to think about it.

He stared at me, but I looked down in shame. He went on, "You were helpless out there. Sometimes I think you get so into your daydreams you forget the world is a dangerous place. Creepers, zombies, spiders. There's so much out there that could kill you."

Another weak nod from me.

"Even on overcast days, if it's dark enough, you might see a zombie!" Dad went on. "And here it was, pitch black out, and you were lying defenseless on the grass."

"It won't happen again," I said.

"You can't make that promise," he said. "Sometimes they take you by surprise. Remember when I was sixteen and the village was attacked? Thank goodness I had my diamond sword."

He nodded to the sword where it was now hanging on the wall—as if I could ever forget that sword.

"I'm not always going to be around to protect you," he said. "I know you're still young and still have training to do, but what happened tonight wasn't about training, it was about common sense."

And then, he said the worst part. "You disappoint me."

He got up from the bed and went into another part of the house, leaving me alone to sit with those words. *You disappoint me.* Somehow these words hurt worse than all the other pain I'd been through that evening.

CHAPTER 4

OSSIE SLEPT NEXT TO ME ALL THROUGH THE NIGHT. She purred as if she knew I needed sympathy and love, but none of this could let me forget Dad's words.

In the morning, Dad made me breakfast and instructed me to rest. He was going to go mining and see if he could find more emeralds to trade with the blacksmith in the village.

I stayed in bed until I got hungry again. It was lunchtime and I was feeling mostly okay by then, but I couldn't stop thinking about the night before. The creeper had done a real number on my tree house—I could only imagine what it looked like today. It had been too dark so I couldn't see all the damage it had done.

I gave Ossie some food, grabbed my tool pouch and headed out to see the tree house.

My tree house was a sad sight: everything I'd done was in pieces, scattered around the area. I sighed. After checking out the situation, I decided I might as well get back to work now. I was still weak enough that I couldn't work too hard, but I was feeling well enough to get some things done.

With my stone pickaxe I began getting more oak wood. The full sun was overhead and I wiped the sweat on my brow. I needed to get a drink and there was a lake not too far away.

I knew the grounds well because I'd followed Dad around since I was little. So when I got near the lake and noticed a portal glowing under a covering of trees, it made me stop in my tracks.

Portals were the gateways from the Overworld into the Nether, a place I'd never gone to without Dad. Too dangerous. Dad had made some of his own portals, putting together the obsidian blocks and the spark of fire in the middle. Those portals looked like black doorways with sizzling purple centers. If you leaped through it, you would be taken to a land of fire and lava.

The thing was, this portal wasn't made of obsidian, and it wasn't glowing purple in the middle, either.

I squatted in front of it, running my hands over the strange rocks. I'd never seen rocks like these before. The middle part was sizzling and glowing with different colors, which was even stranger. Nether portals stayed purple, but this one was rapidly changing from green to blue to red.

Had Dad put this portal together this morning? He was good about teaching me all the things he knew, and he'd never ever mentioned a portal like this. I stared into its pulsing center, to try to detect what lay on the other side.

A part of me really wanted to step through it and find out, though I hesitated. If it was the Nether I could jump right back out. But something told me that if it was a Nether portal, it would have looked like one.

Maybe it's some other realm, I said to myself. Another world sounded nice, a place to go where my dad wasn't mad at me. A place where maybe I could make new friends.

I waded into the fresh water in the lake with my tool pouch on my shoulder. I filled the glass I had with me, but I couldn't keep my eyes off that portal. Even while I was drinking, my eyes zeroed in on it. It almost felt as if the portal was calling to me, as if it wanted me to move forward. Sometimes Dad said he could feel the diamonds calling to him when he was mining. I always thought that sounded impossible until now. He said the diamonds had called out extra loud the day he found the ones he used to make his zombie-killing sword.

I was so caught up in staring at the portal that I didn't see the spider until it was almost too late.

CHAPTER 5

THE SPIDER WAS CHARGING TOWARD ME, RED EYES glowing, hostile under the shade of the trees. Just in time, I yanked my pickaxe out of the tool pouch and sent it flying. The pickaxe hit the spider on one leg and then bounced off. For a second the spider stopped, stunned. And then the mob was coming at me again.

I turned and ran, reaching into my pouch for another weapon. I was struggling to get away, still weak from the creeper attack. The spider advanced toward me, and all the tools I threw at it either missed or bounced ineffectively against its legs. Those red eyes were getting closer and the spider emitted a high hiss. This time there was no one around to save me.

I backed up against the portal, and faced the menacing spider. I knew there was no other choice now. Just as the spider reared up and my entire vision filled with its red eyes, I let myself fall back into the portal.

Right away the red eyes morphed into an entire world of shining red, and then the pulses of light around me turned blue, and then finally everything flared into a giant grass green. I hurtled through the other end of the portal, and landed into a stranger world than I ever could have imagined.

The first thing I knew was that I had landed face down. Ouch. But the ground I was on . . . was fuzzy. And white. And it felt like I was kind of—but not really—sinking into it. And it smelled funny.

Slowly my head tilted up. Was this . . . a bedroom? It kind of looked like my bedroom because there was a bed there, but everything else was all wrong. Everything looked so squishy and there were many different kinds of shapes. Not everything was square, like it should be. And what was up with these dimensions? There was a window nearby, streaming in sunlight.

I didn't know what-in-Overworld I'd stumbled into. Slowly I started to get up, and that's when something in this bedroom-not-a-bedroom let out a shriek. It stood by the door and it looked like some type of humanlike mob I'd never seen before. It wasn't green like a zombie, and it didn't smell bad. It had olive skin and arms and legs like me, but at the end of each of its arms were five things that looked like squid tentacles, only smaller. Its face was oval, its body more distinct than the block shape a human should have had. It had loose tendrils of black stuff coming from the top of its head, but instead of being blocky like real hair, it was wispy and was broken up into thin, silky little pieces like spiderwebs collected in the mines.

This was the mob that had made that horrible screaming sound. It reached behind its pink too-soft-and-squishy-to-be-a-bed bed and pulled out a long, sticklike weapon.

The spider was behind me at the other side of the portal and this mob with a weapon was in front of me. Either way, I was in trouble.

The mob swung the weapon back over its shoulder in a threatening motion, letting me know it would hit me with it. As simple as that weapon was, it looked like it could pack a wallop. I figured it could do a lot more damage than anything in my tool pouch could.

Ever since I was a kid I'd been drilled on the best way to fight and kill mobs. They each had little or big differences. But this mob was my height and glaring at me in direct sunlight—and it looked dangerous. My hand flew to my tool pouch to grab something, anything.

The mob shouted, "What are you doing in my room?"

Mobs could talk like this? I thought, bewildered.

"What are you?" I exclaimed. I yanked out my shovel, the best thing I had left in my tool pouch. But my shovel looked so small and useless next to the mob's weapon.

"What do you mean, 'What am I?!'" it yelled right back. "You came flying out of my computer!"

I didn't know what kind of sorcery a "computer" was, but I had a feeling it wasn't good. And, besides, shouldn't it have been a portal I'd come out of?

"I'll call the police if you even think about hurting me!" the humanlike mob said, its brown eyes flashing.

I didn't know what kind of sorcery "police" was, either.

"I only attack in self-defense," I said, eyeing its weapon. "And you give me good reason to defend myself."

The mob was inching toward a small silver thing on the table next to the not-a-bed. The silver thing had a little screen on it, kind of like a portal, but it was way too small to be a portal and it had little square images on it. "I'm going to do it," she said, "I'm going to call the police."

"I don't know what you're talking about," I said. "And I don't know what kind of mob you are. But you're not hurting me."

"Mob?" it said. Something seemed to dawn in its eyes. It lowered its weapon and I saw it shake a little, but not in the way a creeper shakes.

That shaking made everything fall into place for me. And at the same time I could see from her eyes that everything was falling into place for her.

This wasn't a mob I'd found—it was a human.

CHAPTER 6

"YOU REALLY ARE FROM *MINECRAFT*," SHE GASPED, taking a step back. She'd stopped reaching for the little silver object, but she wasn't getting far away from it, either, as if she wanted to keep it close just in case.

"I come from the Overworld," I protested. "I saw this portal and there was a spider chasing me, so I jumped through."

She was turning reddish. It was weird, but I guess it was better than turning green like a zombie. She sat back on the not-a-bed, shaking her strange oval head, putting her weird squid tentacles against her brow, just below the bizarre wispy, spiderweb hair.

"Did I just create you and make you real?" she whispered.

"Huh?" I said. "No, you didn't create me. I've been alive eleven years."

She set the weapon down on the not-a-bed. "I was playing *Minecraft* on my computer and I found rocks I've never seen before. I Googled them but I couldn't find anything, so I figured they were some new thing to the game. I thought it'd be fun to make a new kind of portal and see if something happened."

I didn't understand half of what she was saying, but I knew she must have been the one who made the portal. And she'd made it all from her own world!

I looked behind me. There was a wooden desk there with . . . a small silver portal? It wasn't very big and it wasn't made of blocks, but it was rimmed with silver and had silver in the back, and inside I could see my world. The spider wandered around as if it was looking for me.

"Is this your portal to the Overworld?" I asked, pointing.

"My portal?" she said in disbelief. "That's my computer!"

"Your portals are called computers?"

For some reason she covered her whole oval face with her squid tentacles. "This can't be real. I must be sleeping."

"This is a very unusual portal," I said. "I've never seen one like it. Do your Nether portals also look like this?"

"There are no Nether portals," she said. "You're a video game character. You're not real. This is a dream. It has to be. Yeah. I never get enough sleep when school starts. So I guess I must have fallen asleep after I finished my homework. Yeah. And I've been playing *Minecraft* so much that I had a dream about it. That's it. And I built a funny portal in my dream and this *Minecraft* character comes flying through my computer screen and lands face-first on my floor, and for some reason I'm not waking up even though I'm pinching myself and it hurts."

She *was* pinching herself. This was a very strange girl.

"There are no portals?" I said, confused. "But how do you get to the Nether?"

"There is no Nether," she said. "Don't you understand what I'm saying?" She grabbed a small thin object that said "*Minecraft*" and had a picture of a guy who looked like me on it. "I bought this at the store to play on my computer."

"I don't understand," I said.

"I don't, either," she said. "Okay, back up. You say you're eleven years old and you just jumped through this portal to get away from a spider?"

"Yes, pretty much," I said. "And I'm still not feeling too well after getting hurt by a creeper, so I couldn't fight that spider. I had to take my chances with the portal. I jumped through the portal and landed on this weird fuzzy stuff."

"A carpet," she said.

"And you were holding a strange weapon."

"A baseball bat," she said.

"And you have stuff like squid tentacles on your hands."

"They're called fingers!" This time she sounded really insulted.

"So what world is this?" I asked.

"Well," she said with a sigh. "That's a good question. Because until two minutes ago, I thought this world was the only world in existence."

CHAPTER 7

THAT GAVE ME A START. SHE COULD SEE INSIDE MY world but for some reason didn't believe in it, even though it was right there before her eyes. She had no idea about portals or anything.

"What's a video game?" I asked.

"It's a game you play," she said. "I build things in *Minecraft*. I make farms and fight mobs. I started a new game today, and every time you start a new game, you get a new area of land. And I saw those rocks and I thought I'd make something different this time."

"You don't have to be scared," I said, because I could see she was trembling. "There are lots of worlds. I grew up knowing that, so it's not scary to me. I guess if you didn't realize it, it probably would be pretty scary when you first learned. Sometimes I go to the Nether with my dad, but this world is brand-new to me." I tucked my shovel back into my tool pouch, aware I wouldn't be needing it.

"I didn't mean to upset you," I continued. "I really was just trying to get away from that spider."

I took another glance back at the "computer." The spider was still wandering around, as clueless as ever. She got up and touched something on the computer and the middle of the computer went completely black. It had turned to night, no moon. I realized the round thing she pushed must have been a button, but it wasn't square like buttons should be.

"And you're still here even with the computer off," she mused. "I guess you really are real."

She looked me over, and I realized I probably looked about as weird to her as she did to me. Then she said, "I'm Maison."

"Stevie," I said.

That got her to smile a little. "Of course," she said. "Stevie."

CHAPTER 8

I T TURNED OUT THE NOT-A-BED REALLY WAS A BED, and we sat there telling each other about ourselves and our worlds. She was eleven, just like me, and she had a lot more to tell me about her world than I had to tell her about mine. I asked if her family also farmed and mined, and she said, "No. I live with my mom, and she's an architect. She works in an office each day. That's like a building where you have computers and, well, you work there."

"Do you live far from your village?" I asked.

"I guess you could say I live in my village," she said, gesturing toward the window. When I peered out of it, my heart just about dropped. It looked so much like my world and yet so different. There were houses lined up in a row, all of them had a slightly unique appearance. There were trees, too, though they didn't look blocky, and the grass might have been strangest of all. Instead of blocks of green, it stuck out of the ground in a lot of little green strands.

When something noisy and even bigger than a giant spider came rushing past us, I ducked down below the window, expecting the worst. It looked as if there were people inside that noisy thing! Maison said, "Um, that's a car. It's a way people get around. I guess it's a little like our version of a Minecart."

Slowly I let my eyes peek just above the bottom of the window. Another "car" came whishing by, and I could definitely see people in it this time. It had wheels at the bottom and was a big, shiny black color.

"Wow," I breathed. "How do those work?"

"You have a steering wheel and gas pedals. Only adults are allowed to drive them, though."

It did look as if those things would make trips to the village much faster for Dad and me.

"I like to ride on pigs," I said. "I put a saddle on the pig and it chases after a carrot I put on a stick." Those cars had passed by fast, but I was pretty sure I didn't see any carrots on sticks being used to make them go.

Maison looked at me funny and had nothing to say. So I changed the subject.

"What's that?" I asked. If I angled right and looked to the side of her house, I could see a building much bigger than all the other houses. "A really good builder must have made that one."

"That's my school, where I go each day to learn with the other kids," she said.

"You mean your mom doesn't teach you?" I said. My whole life, it'd been Dad teaching me everything.

"No," she said. "I have one teacher for shop class, one teacher for English, one for math, one for history, one for science, one for P.E. . . ."

"Oh, wow," I said, because I didn't know what else to say. Mostly because I didn't really follow her. I guessed that "teacher" was the term used for someone who taught you stuff. It sounded like she had a lot of them. "That sounds amazing. Can I see?"

She sucked in a breath. "Well, it's Sunday today so school's closed. But tomorrow is Monday and school starts in the morning."

"Do they teach you how to build tree houses?" I asked eagerly. Maybe I could learn useful new stuff in this world and make a really amazing tree house that would blow Dad's mind.

"No," she said. "They teach you how to do math and spell and stuff like that."

"Do they teach you how to fight mobs?"

"There are no mobs."

"No mobs!" This was the most stunning thing yet. "So you don't have to worry about zombies at night? Or creepers?"

"No, there's nothing like that here. There are spiders, but they're really small and most of them are harmless."

I think my mouth was hanging open. This world may have looked ugly with its strange shapes and people with squid tentacle fingers and spiderweb hair, but there were a lot of nice things about it.

"So you can build without worrying about mobs?" I said.

"Well, most people here don't build," she said. "People like my mom make designs and then construction workers put it together. I want to be an architect when I grow up, too."

"Why don't people build?" *How could they not?* I thought.

"They pay other people to do it."

"With emeralds?"

"No, with money. Uh, here." I watched as she reached into the side of her pants and pulled out several green and white sheets with images and writing on them. "This is money."

"I've never seen anything like this while mining," I said, taking one. It was so light, but it was green like an emerald. "Do you trade it to the blacksmith for all sorts of good stuff?"

"There is no blacksmith," she said. "You go to stores and buy what you want with money. You have to work a job to get the money. You don't go mining for it. There's a factory that makes money."

What an amazing world! "So you don't have to be a good builder to be taken seriously and you don't have to fight mobs?" I said, giving her the money back. In my mind I was thinking I might want to stay here forever. "This sounds like paradise."

"This place isn't paradise," Maison said sadly, looking out the window at the school building. "Far from it."

"How can this world be bad if there are no mobs?" I asked.

Maison leaned back against the wall, blowing a stray bit of hair out of her face. "Because there are eighth graders."

"Eighth graders?" That didn't sound like an especially scary kind of enemy, but I would have to trust her on this. "So they're your version of mobs?"

"I guess," she said. "I finished fifth grade last year, and so now I started middle school. It's a different building with different teachers and all my good friends from elementary school went to the other middle school in town—uh, in the 'village.'"

"Oh," I said. I didn't understand all the terms she was using, but I understood what she was trying to say. "So you don't have friends anymore."

"They said we'd stay in touch, but they lied!" she said. "Now they act too cool for me and they just want to hang out with kids from their new middle school. I ran into them at the mall yesterday—that's like a big market in the village—and they barely even looked at me. They were making fun of me because I had paint splatters on my clothes from something I'd been making. They were all trying on makeup and buying new clothes and . . . and . . . they told me I was stupid and ugly!"

"That's terrible!" I said. I knew how much words could hurt.

"But what are these . . . eighth graders?" I asked, hoping I said it right. She was throwing a lot of new words at me.

"So I'm in sixth grade at middle school and I don't have any friends," she said. "And these two eighth grade guys really like to pick on me. I don't even know why. It's like they chose me on the first day of school to be their punching bag or something. They're making me miserable."

"They try to turn you into a punching bag?" I said. "What kind of sorcery does that involve?"

For some reason that got her to laugh a little. "Oh, Stevie," she said. "I'm just saying they like to upset me. I shouldn't let them get to me, but they do."

"So what you're telling me," I said, "is that they're like creepers? They show up and try to ruin the good things you could have if they weren't there?" I thought about this for a moment. "Do cats scare eighth graders away like they scare away creepers?"

"No," she said. "But I did hear that one of the eighth graders is scared of spiders. Too bad spiders don't get big here, huh?"

"Yeah, huh," I said, even though I thought she was really lucky spiders didn't get big here.

CHAPTER 9

MAISON PUSHED THE BUTTON ON HER COMPUTER portal and brought the Overworld back up in the middle of it. The spider was still there, pacing.

"Great," I groaned. "I was hoping it would have left by now."

"You can spend the night," she said.

I almost said, "I don't want to worry my dad." But then I thought through it. If I went back and told Dad all about this new world, he might forbid me from ever going back. He wasn't big into change.

And that comment about me disappointing him? That still stung, and I flushed thinking about it.

Just one night, I thought. I'll spend the night here, go to school tomorrow to get a better feel of this world, and then go home.

"How about I give you a tour of the place before my mom gets home from work?" Maison said. "Normally she doesn't work on Sundays, but she had to run to the office for something quick. We don't really want her to see you because it'd be too hard to explain."

So she led me around her house. Besides Maison's bedroom, there was a living room, a kitchen, a bathroom, and a bedroom for her mom. It was not as nice as any of the places Dad made, but it had the same sort of rooms. She also said that even though her mom designed houses for work, she hadn't designed her own home. Her mom had bought this house with that green non-emerald stuff that she'd gotten through a factory because she drew buildings on paper. Or at least I think that's what Maison was telling me.

She didn't live on a farm, but she did have some space behind her house that she said was a "backyard." It wasn't very big. Maison said the grass out front was called the "front yard." That made sense, but not much else did.

"So you don't have sheep or anything?" I said. "How do you get your wool?" And then I thought. "Wait, from the stores, right? You really do get mostly everything from the stores, huh?"

"Yes, we do," she said, and looked tired of explaining about the stores again.

Back up in her room, she said, "My mom should be home soon, so I'll go ahead and make you a bed for tonight. I'll be right back."

I sat on the edge of her bed, thinking. *Wait, hadn't Maison said earlier that people didn't actually make stuff in this world?* I didn't want her to have to give her green non-emerald things to a store to get me a bed; I didn't want to be a bother to her like that.

I decided I would make my own bed and save her the trouble. Normally I made a bed out of three planks of wood and some wool, but there were no planks of wood in the house and I didn't know where the store was that sold wool. There were some trees in her backyard, but I couldn't knock them down without asking permission.

There had been a fireplace in the living room, and it had chunks of wood piled next to it. I would have to make do. I got together the firewood, put the pieces on Maison's desk (the closest thing I could see to a crafting table), and got to work.

Maison came back to her bedroom a few minutes later, calling out, "I have blankets!" But then she stopped in the doorway, her eyes going wide. I had just finished up my firewood-made bed.

"Ah, thanks!" I said, taking the blankets she had in her arms. They were so soft! "This will make the bed comfortable."

"I was just going to lie a bunch of blankets on the floor for a bed," she said, kneeling down to check out what I'd made. "This is pretty good, especially since you made it so fast."

Maison ran one of her "fingers" along the edge of my bed. "I would love to build things all the time. You have no idea how lucky you are."

That got me to stop right in the middle of fluffing up blankets. Me, the klutz builder, lucky?

"Here, I want to show you something." She reached into her closet and pulled out a miniature house, all made out of oak wood. I sucked in a breath when I saw it. It looked eerily similar to the tree house I had in mind and had been trying to make. There were definitely different details, like how this was a stand-alone house and not something in a tree, but it was alike enough to make me not want to take my eyes off of it.

"Do you have creatures who can live in there?" I asked.

"No," she said. "It's a model house. I want to show it to my shop class teacher. I worked on it all summer. See?"

She set it down on her desk and lifted the roof off it. Inside I could see tiny furniture.

"I whittled all that furniture from firewood," she said. "This took me months! The one thing I looked forward to with middle school was shop class. But the shop class teacher is so scared we'll get hurt that she never lets us make anything interesting. She always says," Maison puckered up her face and made her voice snooty, "'The shop class room is not a joke! You can get seriously hurt in here. No running. No grabbing. No looking away from what you're doing.'"

"So you can't get hurt in shop class?" I said.

"Well, no, you can," she said. "You need to be careful in shop class, but she's over the top. I want to show her what I can really make. I think a lot of the other kids take shop class to goof around, but I'm serious about this." She put the roof back on her little house.

"You're a builder. What do you think?" she asked.

I thought it was better than anything I could make, but I was too embarrassed to say so. "I think your shop class teacher will love it," I said.

I remained up in Maison's room when her mom got home. While I studied the little house, I listened to Maison and her mom's voices downstairs. I couldn't make out the words, but their conversation sounded pleasant, not at all like my recent talk with Dad.

Sunset came, and for the first time in my life I didn't have thoughts about zombies. I got to sleep in my little firewood bed, a few feet from Maison's bed. Even if zombies couldn't actually get inside a house Dad made, it always turned my stomach to hear them in the distance at night.

But here all I heard was the wind and noises that Maison said came from cars passing by. "And, no," Maison said after I asked, "you do not use carrots on sticks to make cars go."

"Maison," I whispered now, staring out the window.

"What?" she asked sleepily from her bed.

"Your moon is round!" I exclaimed, staring at it.

"Goodnight, Stevie," Maison said, and turned over.

CHAPTER 10

I N THE MORNING MAISON HAD BREAKFAST WITH HER mom. I could hear talking and minutes later Maison returned to her bedroom with my breakfast. She said it was called "cereal" and I needed to eat it with a spoon.

"This is good!" I said, spooning more into my mouth. "How do you make it?"

"The milk comes from a cow, and the cereal comes from grains," she said. She couldn't tell me anything beyond that, which was weird, because I knew exactly where all my food came from. While I slurped down my breakfast, she went over to the computer portal and pressed the button. Within a minute, my world was back on her computer again. No sign of the spider.

That probably means I should go back home, I thought, biting at my spoon. I no longer had the excuse of needing to stay here to keep me safe from the mob.

But I really didn't want to go back, not till I saw the school and learned a little more about this world.

"I still have a hard time believing all this." Maison shook her head as she stared through the computer portal. "Playing video games will never be the same again."

She put a bag over her shoulders and said it was called a "backpack," but told me to leave my tool pouch here, because some of the stuff I had in there wouldn't be "appropriate" to take to school. I had to trust her on that one.

"My mom hasn't left for work yet so we have to be quiet," Maison said, whispering. We made our way down the stairs as quietly as possible and were halfway through the living room when I heard a woman's voice call from the kitchen, "Maison, are you heading out already?"

"Yeah, Mom," Maison said hurriedly.

"I don't get a goodbye first?" Maison's mom said. We heard her footsteps heading our way.

Before I could respond, Maison pushed me into a closet and shut the door. It was really dark in there. Musty, too.

I heard Maison's mom enter the living room and say, "Have fun at school, honey. And if those boys give you any more trouble . . ."

"Mom!" Maison said, sounding embarrassed.

"I'm serious," Maison's mom said. "If I hear one more story about those eighth grade boys harassing you, I'm setting up a meeting with the principal."

The mustiness of the closet was really getting to me. I could feel a sneeze coming on.

"Do you know what happened to the last kid whose mom talked to the principal about bullies?" Maison demanded. "The bullies got off scot-free, but the kid sure didn't. The bullies knew he'd squealed and they went after him."

I couldn't hold it back any longer. I sneezed.

There was a moment of silence in the living room.

"What was that?" Maison's mom asked.

"I didn't hear anything," Maison said quickly.

"It sounded like a sneeze."

Footsteps made their way toward the closet. I tried to back up farther into the closet but there was no place to go. If Maison's mom opened that door, she'd be staring right at me.

"Look, Mom," Maison said. "What do you think of my house?"

The distraction worked. Maison must have been showing off the little house she'd made, because her mother gasped and said, "Oh, it really is amazing! I can't wait for your teacher to see it."

"Don't you have an important meeting today?" Maison asked. "Is all your paperwork ready?"

"Ah, yes," her mom said. "Nothing gets past you, does it?"

I could hear her mom's footsteps walking away. I waited, barely breathing, still so embarrassed by my sneeze. Maison opened the closet door, and said, "Let's go!"

This time we made it out the front door without any problems.

Outside it was raining lightly and Maison opened something called an "umbrella" up over us. She carefully balanced her little house in her arms. Dad had made a lot of impressive stuff, but he'd never thought of making an umbrella so we could walk in the rain without getting wet.

"I'm really sorry about sneezing," I said.

"It's okay," she said. "We worked it out."

Well, that was being kind of nice. She'd worked it out, not me. I'd just stayed in the closet and tried not to sneeze again.

"I hope it doesn't rain all day," she said, already over the scare of being found out by her mom. "In P.E. we're supposed to play baseball, but we can't if it rains. You'd love baseball! I'm really good at it, especially at batting. That's why I have the baseball bat."

"You mean that thing wasn't a weapon?" I said, thinking back on how threateningly she'd held it when I'd first kerplunked into her room.

"No," she said. "It's for playing sports. You know, it's for fun."

But her spirits drooped as we neared the school building. There were a ton of other kids walking into the building, and it was a feast for my eyes. It was so crowded it was almost like its own little village. No one was blocky like me, and every single one of them had fingers on the edges of their hands. They all looked much more like Maison than me, except each person had at least slightly different skin and hair colors. They also had diverse body shapes—no square shapes, though. They all had backpacks hanging off their shoulders, and some of them were carrying books in their arms.

I couldn't help staring at them, and then I noticed they couldn't help staring at me. Some kids would glance over, do a double-take, and then look away as if they didn't want to appear rude. Others stared openly, their eyes getting bigger.

"How are we going to explain me to them?" I whispered to Maison. If she'd been too scared to let her mom see me, I didn't know how she was going to handle a whole building full of people.

"Don't worry," she said. "I have it covered."

But it turned out we did have something to worry about. Just as we were reaching the steps of this giant building, two mobs stepped right in front of us, blocking our way.

CHAPTER 11

I COULD TELL FROM MAISON'S PANICKED FACE THAT THE two tough-looking boys in front of us must be the eighth graders she'd told me about. They basically looked like regular kids (I mean, regular for this world), except they were bigger and taller than us, which made me think of tall Endermen. I had to crane my head back to see their faces. These two looked a lot stronger than both Maison and me, and their smiles didn't make me feel at all good about the situation.

"Well, well, well, what do we have here, Dirk?" asked the one on the left.

"I don't know, Mitch," the one on the right said with a smirk.

"Move out of the way," Maison said. "You're blocking our way and it's raining."

"Why, does rain make you melt?" teased Mitch.

"It might make this one melt." Dirk pointed a finger my way. "He doesn't look right."

"Yeah, what's wrong with this blockhead?" Mitch said. "Does he need a hospital?"

"He's my cousin," Maison said. "He's visiting the school today, and he has a rare food allergy that makes him swell up and get squarish. So don't be rude and make fun of people for their allergies."

Dirk and Mitch exchanged Did-I-Hear-That-Right? glances.

"I don't know," Mitch said. "He kinda looks like he's from that video ga—"

"Now move," Maison repeated, interrupting him before he could finish his thought. She tried to walk past them, but as she did, Dirk reached out and snatched up her house.

"What's this?" he said in a baby voice. "A li'l doll house for your Bratz?"

"Give that back!" Maison exclaimed, trying to grab it. Dirk held it out of her reach and tossed it over to Mitch.

"Oh, look, the roof comes off," Mitch said, pulling the small roof aside to look. "And it's got cute little furniture!"

"Aww," Dirk wheezed. "Mind if we play with it for a bit?"

"That isn't yours!" She tried to grab the house again and failed because Mitch raised it up so high neither one of us could reach it. All I could do was stand there and stare—she was right, this wasn't at all like the mobs back home. These guys were *enjoying* upsetting her.

"You like baseball, right?" Mitch said. "We saw you playing after school the other day."

"Hey, yeah, she was a pretty good little batter," Dirk said. "Let's see how good of a catcher she is."

"Catch!" Mitch called, and sent the little house flying toward the school building. Maison cried out and ran after it. But her attempt to save it was pointless, and the house smashed into pieces against the school building, the bits of furniture scattered around it.

Mitch and Dirk laughed in a way that sounded much worse than any noise a zombie could make. "Whoops, looks like you need more practice there!" Dirk hooted.

"See ya, blockhead!" Mitch called to me, and the two of them ran off into the safety of the building.

Some of the other kids had watched this happen, but now they all looked away. I realized none of them were going to step forward and help Maison. She was in this alone.

No, I thought. *I'm in this with her.*

She knelt before the broken pieces of her house, gathering a door here and a chair there. I could tell from her face how much she was struggling not to cry.

"Maison," I said, crouching next to her.

"They're awful!" she said, and then she was crying for real. "This is what they do every day and no one stops them!"

"Can you hit them with a sword and make them go away?" I asked, at a loss. "They kind of remind me of Endermen because they're so tall. One time my dad was fighting an Enderman with his diamond sword and—"

"No, they're not like Endermen and you can't hit them with a sword!" she interrupted sharply. "This isn't like your world. You can't just swing a diamond sword here and make everything better. You can be violent in video games, but not for real!"

I reached out and began to help her pick up the pieces. "We can put this back together," I said. "I'll help you. You know, just the other day I was working really hard on a tree house, and a creeper destroyed basically the whole thing."

With the broken pieces in our arms, we stepped into the school. I glanced around, and saw even more kids with even more backpacks. I also noticed how the walls were lined with little doorways that kids were opening and closing. The little doorways had books inside and kids were either putting more books in or taking some out. All this kind of reminded me of chests where Dad and I would keep our stuff, but I knew that couldn't be right. Chests in the Overworld were square and brown and weren't attached to the wall like whatever these doorways were.

I would have asked Maison what was going on with all those doorways but I knew now wasn't the time. She was way too upset. Maison led me to one of those doorways, turned a little knob on it, and opened the door with a sharp clanging noise. She dropped her house pieces in there so I put my pieces in there, too, wanting to help.

"That house took me months," she said, rubbing at her wet face.

I wasn't very good at saying comforting things. It's not like I exactly learned how from Dad, you know?

But I wanted to say something that would make her feel better. As I opened my mouth to try, the school building let out a roar and I jumped straight into the air.

Some of the other kids sighed but none of them panicked like me. Maison remarked blandly, "That bell means class starts in five minutes." She slammed her doorway shut and turned to storm down the hallway. Helpless, I trotted along behind her.

CHAPTER 12

MAISON TURNED INTO A ROOM THAT SMELLED strongly of wood chips. There were several long tables laid out with kids our age sitting there. I let my eyes scan the room, noting the machinery along the back walls. This didn't look anything like the tools I used at home to build. No pickaxes or shovels or swords in sight.

There was someone at the front of the room, sitting behind a desk. "That's the teacher," Maison said and led me to her.

"Ms. Reid," Maison said to the teacher, "is it all right if my cousin Stevie visits the school today?"

I was surprised she didn't say anything about Dirk and Mitch. I was also surprised that Ms. Reid didn't say anything about how Maison had clearly just been crying. Ms. Reid looked up from her desk, did the usual double-take on me, then quickly tried to act as if everything was normal. But she was still flustered.

Maison told Ms. Reid the same story she'd told Dirk and Mitch about my allergy. "Stevie has a very rare allergy that sometimes makes him puff up and look blocky," she said. "But he doesn't like to talk about it, because it makes him feel different from the other kids."

"Oh! Oh, dear!" Ms. Reid said. "Yes, I understand. But are you sure he's all right?"

Maison cleared her throat loudly. I said, "Yes, I'm all right. I just ate something that didn't agree with me. You know, some bad mushroom stew."

"I suppose it would be okay for the day," Ms. Reid mused. "Do you take shop class at your school?"

"I don't go to school," I said.

Ms. Reid was taken aback for some reason. "You don't go to school?"

"What he means is that his dad homeschools him," Maison said.

"Ah, I see," the woman said. "Have you ever worked on equipment like this?"

"No," I said. "But I build a lot of stuff with my dad. The other day I was working on a tree house."

"A tree house!" Ms. Reid said. "Well, that's much more advanced than anything we do here. Maison is a really good student, so I want you to stick with her. But don't touch any equipment without me there. You can get seriously hurt in this room if you're not taking it seriously. Do you see that saw over there? Why, if you're not careful, you could lose a fing—" She stopped herself.

The school roared again and I jumped. Ms. Reid smiled and said, "I guess they don't use bells in homeschooling, hmm? Why don't you two take a seat?"

As I followed Maison to a desk, Ms. Reid said she was happy to see us all for another week and she wanted everyone to meet me, Maison's cousin Stevie. She said, "And remember, we treat all students equally." I think she was telling the kids not to make fun of me or stare at me for my "allergy."

"We're going to have an assembly in a little bit so the principal can talk to you about safety," Ms. Reid said. "But in the meantime, I'd like you to all work on your projects."

After she said that, everyone got to work. Maison bent over a design she was sketching and I whispered to her, "Why didn't you tell her about Dirk and Mitch?"

"Because that never does any good," she said. "They'd maybe get detention and they'd know I told and they'd do worse to me."

In the Overworld, once you defeated a mob, it was over, but I guessed eighth graders just kept coming back.

"Is detention like being stabbed with a sword?" I asked, trying to picture it.

Maison opened her mouth to answer, but then Ms. Reid swooped over me, saying, "Stevie, why don't you come with me and I'll show you around the classroom?"

She took me to a table that had a silver circle in the middle of it. "This is a table saw, Stevie," she said. When a button was pressed, the circle spun so fast it glimmered.

Then she put a block of wood up against it and I watched as the block split evenly in two.

"Wow!" I said, amazed. "That's like a really fast blade!" I grabbed a bigger piece of wood next to the table saw.

"Yes, I suppose that's one way of looking at it," Ms. Reid chuckled, as if I'd said something funny. But her eyes widened in horror when I put the piece of wood against the flashing silver. "Stevie, no!" she exclaimed.

"What?" I asked, holding up the wooden sword I'd made.

"That's—but—you—it's—how—I—." She couldn't get a single real sentence out.

Maison jumped up next to my side. "Stevie, maybe you should come sit with me," she suggested loudly.

"Yes," Ms. Reid said, dazed. "Yes, I think that's enough for today, Stevie."

"But I haven't seen the rest of the room," I protested. Maison grabbed me by the shirt and dragged me to her desk. Ms. Reid was still gaping in the background.

"People can't make stuff that fast in this world!" Maison hissed in my ear. "You're going to give yourself away! It isn't like *Minecraft* here."

"It's not?" I said. But when I sat down and watched how the other kids worked, I realized she was right. They were unbelievably slow—no wonder people here didn't build everything!

"You can't just jump in and use the table saw like that," Maison was explaining. "It's not just that you're too fast. You also don't have the training and could have gotten hurt. That's why Ms. Reid was so upset."

"Oh." I glanced at Ms. Reid, who stared at me from her big desk at the front of the room. She was gripping her desk as if she were afraid to let go of it, her eyes big and scared. To avoid her gaze, I put my head down and began cleaning my sword in my shirt. Back home you made a wooden sword with a stick and two planks of wood, though that table saw had let me carve out a sword from a single piece of wood, which was pretty interesting.

But then Maison looked kind of guilty for getting on my case. "I hope I didn't sound mean or anything," she said. "You just have to be careful here."

"No, you didn't sound mean," I said. "My dad, on the other hand . . ."

She was concerned. "What about your dad?"

"Oh, he just never has anything nice to say," I said, playing with the sword in a fidgety sort of way. I hoped she couldn't tell her question made me uncomfortable. "He's always disappointed in me for one reason or another. When he was twelve, he made a diamond sword that he still uses to slay zombies."

I looked down at my sword. "And a little wooden toy sword is the best I know how to do."

"I think it's a very nice sword," Maison said proudly. "I bet you could get lots of zombies with that."

I laughed, but I knew she was just trying to make me feel better.

"My dad saved my life the other day because I couldn't handle what was going on around me," I said. "You know that creeper I told you about? I just froze when it showed up. I couldn't do anything. The creeper blew up the tree house I'd been making and I got hurt pretty bad. Then six zombies came out of nowhere. My dad had to come out and save me. But afterward, he didn't even act happy that I was okay. He was just mad at me for not doing a better job." This last part was hard to get out. "He said he's disappointed in me."

"Oh, Stevie," she said sympathetically. "It sounds like he's much worse than a creeper any day."

CHAPTER 13

AFTER WE'D BEEN WORKING ON OUR PROJECTS FOR a while, Ms. Reid seemed to come out of her daze.

"Kids," she said. "It's time to line up for the principal's assembly on safety."

"Assembly" was another word I didn't know, so I cast a glance toward Maison. She explained, "We're all going to sit in the auditorium, which is a really big room, and listen to the principal lecture us about being safe. The principal is who's in charge of the school. It's going to be boring."

Judging by the already bored looks of the other kids, she knew what she was talking about. I slipped my wooden sword into my waistband and lined up by the door with the others.

The auditorium was made up of rows and rows of fold-out chairs and there was a giant stage and podium at the front. Maison and I sat next to each other in fold-out chairs in the first row with Ms. Reid and the other kids from shop class sitting around us. There were a few doors but no windows in this big room, and I looked around the crowd, interested in seeing how all the other kids looked. The way the chairs folded up and out was pretty fun, too. Dad had never made anything like this.

But then Maison gasped and I glanced over. Farther down the front row sat Dirk and Mitch, who began to smirk and wave at us. Mitch wrung his hands out next to his eyes, miming a crying gesture and Dirk pointed at Maison and laughed.

My hand itched to go to my sword. Instead, I said, "Can we tell Ms. Reid about them now?"

"No," Maison hissed back. "It won't do any good."

She tried not to look at them, but I noticed her sneak a few peeks from the corners of her eyes. Dirk and Mitch noticed each time she did this, and they always made a show for her, pointing and fake-crying.

A grown woman stepped up to the podium and said something into a black object that was in front of her. Kids started yelling that they couldn't hear, so she moved the black object, causing loud pops to ring out through the room. I jumped.

"That's a microphone," Maison whispered to me. "She just hasn't adjusted it right, which is why we're getting that popping sound."

"How does that work?" But before Maison could answer, the woman on stage spoke again, her mouth closer to the microphone, and this time her voice echoed from every side of the room. This made me *really* jump.

"Boys and girls," she said, "now that we're entering the second month of our new school year, I want to say how pleased I am to have all of you present. We're going to have a great year, but we can't do that without putting safety first. As you know . . ."

Most of the other kids did look bored. But I was fascinated, and enjoyed learning more about how this world worked. *Look both ways before you cross the street. Never leave a science experiment unattended. Don't get into strangers' cars.* So this was the kind of stuff people in Maison's world worried about instead of mobs.

Most of the kids were quiet and listening, but now and then I could hear a hoarse giggle and I'd look over to see Dirk and Mitch. They'd be talking to themselves and cracking up about one thing or another. As soon as they'd see me looking at them, they'd start making fun of Maison again. Finally I decided I wouldn't let myself look in their direction, no matter how loud they got, because I didn't want them upsetting Maison.

I think the principal also noticed Dirk and Mitch, because a few times she'd stop her talk to say, "Everyone, please be quiet." But she never called out anyone's names.

Still, she seemed to get more annoyed as her lecture went on. Finally she said, "Okay, boys and girls, I've had about enough. This is an important lesson that will keep all of you safe, but you're not taking it seriously. I have some of you talking to your friends. I have some of you with your eyes closed. And I have some of you who are looking like total zombies!"

"Hey, *psst, psst,* Stevie!" came a half-garbled, giggly whisper from down the front row. Despite my promise to myself, I glanced over. My mouth fell open. Dirk and Mitch were almost in hysterics, pointing to the two zombies sitting next to them.

"Looks like they've got food allergies, too!" Mitch snickered.

"Only theirs must be worse," Dirk said, pinching his nose. "They're all green and they smell awful!"

Maison glanced over and let out a horrified gasp. She and I were frantically gesturing for Dirk and Mitch to get out of their seats and get away before it was too late. Our fear only made Dirk and Mitch laugh more.

That's when one zombie reached out and grabbed Mitch, whose giggle turned into a high pitched squeal of terror. The zombie knocked him to the floor and lunged at him, emitting a shrieking hiss that echoed throughout the whole auditorium.

CHAPTER 14

J UST LIKE THAT, I WAS OUT OF MY SEAT. EVERYTHING was in slow motion, but instead of being frozen like I was with the creeper, my body instantly responded.

The zombie was barreling down on a screaming, panicked Mitch as I ran up, drawing my sword from my waistband.

"Help!" Mitch cried out, too hysterical to fight back. The zombie was looming right over him, reaching out with green arms. I lifted the sword high above my head and slammed it down on the zombie.

The second zombie had opened his mouth, moaning, and reached out to seize an equally panicked Dirk. I swung my sword to the side, knocking the zombie across the head. It flew from its seat to the floor.

All around me the auditorium exploded with cries and screams as people jumped up from their seats, terrified. The principal called for some kind of order but no one was listening. Before my eyes both zombies slowly rose to their feet, their mouths hissing, their attention on me. While Dirk and Mitch hunched trembling, the zombies advanced toward their new goal.

I swung out wildly. Coming up beside me, Maison leapt into action too and delivered a hard kick into the gut of the second zombie. Our attacks only momentarily stunned the zombies, because the next second the mobs were coming at us again. I swung my sword once more, hit the zombie, and watched it fall back. Without any hesitation Maison delivered another hard kick to the zombie in front of her. Together we knocked the two zombies back and they disappeared into thin air, as if they'd never been there to begin with. And then we stood there, panting, trying to catch our breaths. That was when we finally got a chance to stop and actually think about what had just happened.

I believe we both had a very cold chill go up our spines. I know I felt that chill go up mine. Maison and I stared at each other in horror and we both whispered, "The portal!"

She covered her face with her hands. "I left the computer on this morning! They must be slipping out through there!"

"Do mobs work differently in this world?" I asked, wondering how they could be out and about during the day. And then it hit me. The rain! It was overcast enough that they weren't being burned up by the sun!

"If there are two there might be more," I said.

"What do we do?" she said, glancing down at where the zombies had vanished.

"We need to get my dad," I said. "He's got the diamond sword. He can handle this. He can help us look for any more mobs that might have gotten out."

"You have a sword—" she began.

"No, a real sword!" I said sharply.

"What on earth were those things?" Mitch wailed in the background, his arms still over his head like a shield.

"We have to explain to everyone," Maison said, and just like that she took off, running up onto the stage. The principal was still trying and failing to get everyone's attention, and Maison more or less jumped in front of the podium. She said into the microphone, "Nobody panic! Those were zombies, but we have it under control!"

"Zombies!" the principal shouted. She didn't look as if she fully believed Maison, but she didn't look as if she could un-believe it, either.

"You guys all play *Minecraft*, right?" Maison continued. There were lots of nods in the audience. "Well, somehow a portal has been opened to the *Minecraft* world and that's how the zombies got through. That's really where Stevie came from, too. But everyone, just sit down and remain calm. Stevie and I are going to go back into *Minecraft* and get this taken care of."

"Stay!" Dirk jumped up in outrage. "Forget that! I'm out of here!"

"No!" Maison cried into the microphone, her voice throbbing throughout the room.

Dirk ignored her. He jumped to his feet and ran to the nearest exit, throwing open the heavy doors. But if he meant to save himself, he'd done the absolute worst thing. Once he'd opened the doors and saw the giant, red-eyed spider waiting right there for him, he let out a scream.

CHAPTER 15

MORE MOBS HAD COME THROUGH THE PORTAL! There was no time for me to get sick or sit there and think about how bad this was.

Dirk had fallen back, one arm raised in a pathetic gesture of defense. I came charging toward the spider, hoisting my sword over my head. With great force, I brought the sword down.

The spider roared and drew back, but it hadn't given up. Behind it I could see more spiders stalking forward on their eight black legs. And just behind them was a cluster of zombies, lurching in the direction of the auditorium. They were *everywhere*.

"Maison! There are more!" I yelled, swinging my sword back at the spider. It dodged, pulling away, then came crushing forward, almost nailing me. I'd leapt to the side in the nick of time so that the spider brushed against me instead of hitting me straight on.

I didn't have time to look back, but the next instant I heard her voice. "Block off the other doors!" she called. "Don't let any more get in!"

It was too late. I heard a sickening sound coming from the next door on this side of the auditorium. There was no time for me to run there and do anything. Someone was smashing against the wooden door, breaking it. Spiders couldn't break through doors, though zombies could, and unless someone did something, they were going to break through at any moment. But no one knew how to respond and time was against us, anyway. The door burst to pieces and several zombies staggered through the wreckage.

"We're doomed!" Dirk cried, grabbing my shirt and clinging to me. "You can keep them back, right? Right!"

"Let go!" I tried to push him off. Keeping this spider at bay was hard enough without Dirk grabbing me. But who was I fooling? I knew it was only a matter of time before all the spiders swarmed in on me. The people in this world had no idea how to handle mobs, and I had proven I couldn't handle a few of them, let alone this many.

"Everyone, it's just like *Minecraft!*" Maison's voice blared. "Grab things that can work as weapons and hit them back! They're only attacking this side of the auditorium, so someone go out the other side and get baseball bats from the gym! Someone get out their cell phone and call the police! Hurry!"

She leapt off the stage, landing square on the spider, giving the final blow needed to defeat it. But there was no time to say thanks—the next spider crawled over to replace it, rearing up at me.

"Dirk!" Maison said. "Get up and help us fight!"

"I can't!" he wailed.

The other kids didn't feel that way, though. They were standing in droves to fight back, hitting the spiders and then the zombies with whatever they had on them. Books and backpacks were being used as weapons because that's all that was available. Off to the side Ms. Reid had a little silver object to her face and was shouting, "911! I'm at the middle school and there are zombies and huge spiders attacking . . . yes, you heard right!"

As much as the kids were trying to help, there wasn't much they could do. Even if they played video games, that wasn't the same as staring directly into the eyes of an attacking mob. Plus they didn't have any real weapons. The kids were hitting back with their backpacks, smashing up against the mobs as hard as they could. But the mobs were barely taking any damage. And if anyone was seriously injured or died, it would be my fault.

"Yes, I said 'zombies!'" Ms. Reid was still screaming in the background, yet I could barely hear her, even though she was a few feet away. The auditorium was taken up by moans and hisses from zombies and spiders.

Slamming my sword down and finishing off the spider in front of me, I thought desperately. We needed to get this situation at the auditorium under control. Once that was done, Maison and I could run back to her house and go through the portal. We'd get Dad, and he would have his sword if there were any other mobs in this world. Once all the mobs were taken care of, we'd close the portal.

Maybe Dad would have to get some of the villagers to come help, too, but the point was he would know how to handle everything. He and his sword. That sparkling diamond sword that my little shop class sword couldn't hold a candle to.

"Maison!" I yelled above the uproar as I dodged the front claws of the latest spider. "We need to close the portal!"

She must have heard me, because the next instant she was by my side. "Give me your sword!" she yelled. "I'm good at *Minecraft*! I'll hold this door off while you make more weapons. There are trees just outside past the doors on the other side of the auditorium—run!"

There was no time to argue. In a moment I passed the sword over and she clutched it in her sweaty fingers, thrusting it deep at the spider and causing it to disappear.

"Maison, Maison, I'm sorry I ever teased you!" Dirk shouted, still on the floor, still cowering.

When the next spider swiped out at her, Maison took a step back, dodging. She stepped on Dirk and he wailed out. I know she hadn't meant to step on him, but I think I might have seen a little smile on her face.

Meanwhile, I was charging toward the closest door on the other side of the auditorium.

I threw the door open, holding my breath, ready for there to be another crowd of mobs. But here I could only see clear space and a light mist. And trees. Lots of trees.

The rain had stopped, and I hoped that meant the cloud covering would go away soon, too. However, there was no sense in sitting around waiting for the sun to break through the clouds. I began knocking down blocks from the trees as quickly as I could. Tree punching was a simple and speedy way to get weapons. Kids saw what I was doing and were snatching the tree blocks up as soon as they hit the ground. They went charging back into the auditorium. The principal came running out, too, grabbing a block. Before returning to the chaos to help the fight, she said, "I don't know who you are, young man, but I thank you."

And back into the building she went.

I'd made those blocks of wood because they were the fastest weapon I could think of and they could help the kids immediately. But tree blocks weren't the best weapons—they were only a little better than backpacks. You had to hit a zombie or spider a lot to get anything done with them.

So I switched gears. With a few planks of wood I made a crafting table, and now that I had a table, I could make real weapons. Fast as can be, I was churning out wooden swords and handing them off to kids. They weren't diamond swords, but they were the best I could do right then, and I was making them in the Overworld style, with a stick and two wooden planks. No table saw here. Kids were snatching up the wooden swords by the handles and going in after the mobs.

Ms. Reid came out of the building, yelling hysterically into her silver object. "You heard me! I said there are zombies and spiders and they're attacking the middle school! This is not a joke!" She must have seen me making swords just as swiftly as I had with the table saw, but this time she didn't even blink at it.

"The police don't believe us," a kid gasped as he seized the latest wooden sword I'd made. "We're all on our own for this."

"We just have to push them back," I said, almost out of breath from exertion. "Once we do that, I'll get my dad, who's the best mob fighter all around."

But I didn't know how long it would take before we could push them back. If we could.

Across the lawn a group of kids came running toward us, holding piles of sticks in their hands. No, wait, baseball bats! I recognized them from what Maison had in her room.

"Great, take them inside!" I said. I'd fully turned three trees into blocks and swords the kids could use. With all those weapons and now these baseball bats, I dashed back inside to see how things were going in the auditorium.

A few kids had been hurt, but nothing too bad. Maison was back on stage, using the microphone to call out directions. Like a general she was watching everything going on in the room.

"Jeremy, zombie to your left!" she called. "Good! Dalton, use your block over the spider's head. Right! Tobias, behind you—good job!"

As I ran back to where I started, she tossed my sword down to me. I caught it by the handle, and for the briefest second Maison smiled at me. It wasn't an "Everything is better" smile, because even though we'd made some headway, things were definitely not all better. But it was a "We're in this together" sort of smile.

And that sort of smile was all we had time for. With the shop class sword in my hand again, I jumped over Mitch's shaking, cringing body and hit back a zombie. The zombie moaned, shook itself, came at me again.

Maison leapt back down beside me.

"Are there any diamond mines around?" I called out, but I was pretty sure I already knew the answer.

"No," she said, kicking at a spider.

"Ahhh! I hate spiders!" Dirk was weeping. "All those legs!"

As I pulled back my sword for a final hit, I was startled to see Ms. Reid jump in, knocking the zombie soundly with one of the wooden swords I'd made. The zombie vanished.

"Good job, kids," Ms. Reid said. "I think I finally convinced the police—they said they're on their way! And Stevie, you can make swords in my shop class class any day."

"What are the police?" I asked. I imagined them like the iron golems who protected the village, only softer and less blocky. Would they storm into the school and take out the rest of the mobs?

"The police will help, but we need to close the portal!" Maison said. "That's the only way because otherwise the mobs will keep coming!"

She was right. I looked around the room, checking out the situation. The majority of the mobs had been destroyed, and the few left were being pushed back through the doors.

"I got it!" I said. "We need to push the rest of the mobs out, then barricade the doors. Spiders can't open doors, but zombies can, so the barricades will keep them out. Then the kids can stay safe in here until the police come."

"I'm on it!" Ms. Reid said, running to the other door and telling the kids what they needed to do. Shutting the doors would be harder for them because of the damage the zombies had done. But if they pushed back and got enough stuff blocking the doorway, it would work.

"We have to close this door," I told Maison.

"The police won't know how to handle the mobs," she said.

"Then I'll go out there and tell them," I said. "And then I'll run back to the portal."

"I'm coming with you," she said.

CHAPTER 16

I N A MATTER OF SECONDS MAISON WAS BACK ON STAGE giving directions. "Everyone, we're going to push the mobs out and barricade the doors!" she said. "The police are on their way and they'll be able to help us. We just need to stay safe until then."

The mention of the police, whatever they were, seemed to give everyone some relief. They pushed back even harder, knowing this was the last bit of work they had to do. I tried to calm my beating heart—I knew my work was far from over.

As we destroyed or pushed out the last few mobs, I heard a rhythmic wailing sound from outside, rising and falling. Kids were shouting, "The police! The police!"

The last few mobs at the other door were pushed out. Kids took their tree blocks and barricaded the heavy door, hearing the *skreech*, *skreech* of spider legs rubbing against it on the other side.

I looked at the door by me, where a few zombies were trying to climb in. "Get ready," I said to Maison. "Let's go!"

Together she and I knocked the zombies back, pushing them out of the doorway. The auditorium door slammed shut behind us, and I could hear a hasty barricade being made. The kids and the teachers were safe. But now Maison and I were on our own.

Maison knocked back at the zombies with her tree block and I sliced with my sword, half-aware of several cars zooming up close, flashing red and blue on their tops. Men and women in blue clothing were jumping out of the cars, shouting "Freeze!"

This was the police? They didn't look like iron golems at all. They must not have ever played *Minecraft*, either, because they didn't know that zombies and spiders wouldn't follow orders.

"Help the kids inside the auditorium!" Maison called out to them. She gave a zombie one last good hit and the police all gaped as the zombie went away before their eyes.

"They're zombies and spiders from *Minecraft*!" she continued. "You have to hit them with things."

At first the police looked as if they couldn't believe what she was saying, just like the principal hadn't believed her. But as they watched what was going on, they couldn't *not* believe, either. The police rushed in, helping us take care of the remaining swarm of mobs around the auditorium. They had little wooden sticks they were using to hit back, not as good as baseball bats, but something. Even though the police weren't iron golems, they were as determined as we were to get the job done.

"I thought the woman on the phone was playing a prank!" I heard one member of the police say as she hit out at a zombie with her stick. "But it's all true!"

When the last zombie vanished and the final spider fell backward and disappeared, the police looked ready to cheer. They threw open the auditorium doors to help the kids out and make sure they were okay.

Maison and I looked at each other, trying to catch our breaths. The police, kids, and teachers all thought everyone was safe now. They didn't realize that as long as that portal was open, more mobs would be able to get out. What if a creeper sneaked out and blew everything sky high?

"Let's go!" I said to Maison, even though we hadn't fully caught our breaths yet. The police, kids, and teachers were too caught up in what was going on to notice us rush toward Maison's house.

And it was just as we suspected. Another zombie came prowling around her porch as soon as we were rounding the corner into her yard. Her wooden front door had been smashed to pieces. Behind this zombie lurched another one, the two of them moaning on and off as they approached us.

"I got it!" I said, nailing the first zombie while Maison went after the second one. Deeper in the house we could hear more moans and hisses.

"Stevie," Maison said as she fought, "how do we close the portal?"

I didn't answer. I just kept fighting the zombie.

And it's not because I didn't know the answer. I did. It just wasn't an answer I wanted to think about.

There was only one way to close the portal.

We would have to destroy it.

I would have to go into my home world and take the portal apart, piece by piece. It would keep any more mobs from going through into Maison's world. It would save countless lives.

But it would also destroy any connection I had to this world. I would never be able to return.

I would never see Maison again.

CHAPTER 17

"**W**E'RE ALMOST THERE!" MAISON PANTED AS WE battled back through the mobs. There were six of them in the living room, reeling on their dead, unsteady feet. "We're almost to the portal!"

There were more items in the house that could be used as weapons, so Maison tossed aside the clunky block of wood and began to grab other things. When a spider came charging into the room and reared at her, she easily ducked back over the couch, saving herself. The spider began to crawl over the couch to investigate, but when it reached the cushions, Maison jumped up from the other side, swinging the poker from the fireplace. The spider flipped back and was gone.

Maison stepped back into a corner so no mobs could sneak up behind her. She was holding out her poker as if daring them to come close. The zombies either turned toward her or turned toward me.

I felt the mobs closing in on me and I kept slashing away, too consumed with staying alive to look over at how Maison was doing. If I glanced away even for a second, it could be the end of me. It would probably be the end of her, too, because then she'd have to take on all of the mobs instead of half.

I had to trust that she knew what she was doing, and judging by everything that had happened so far, she did. I slashed out at the zombies as hard and fast as I could, needing to take care of them so I could see Maison. *Slam. Slash.* A zombie was gone. Another one reared up. *Bam!* My sword knocked it back a step.

I went after another zombie, and when that one got knocked back, I went after another. Enough hits and they were gone. My sword was a blur. When all the mobs in my area of the living room were destroyed, I looked over at Maison, and she was using her poker to finish off the last zombie in her group. A strong jab with her poker and the mob was gone. She appeared relieved for a second and then panicked.

"My mom's going to kill me!" Maison screamed, looking around at the torn-apart living room. "Look at this mess."

I didn't think that would be true at all. Maison's mom sounded nice when I heard her talking the night before. My *dad* was the person to be scared of—and it wouldn't be too much longer before I'd have to come face-to-face with him and explain what happened. Running away without telling him, entering a whole new world, letting mobs into that whole new world . . . this day was just going to keep getting worse.

With the mobs in the living room defeated, we rushed throughout the house, looking for any more mobs that might be there. My skin crawled, expecting to have a mob jump at me from around a corner. I didn't hear any more hissing or moaning, but somehow the silence was even scarier. If there were more, they were doing a good job at hiding. And they might get us before we had a chance to get them.

I looked over at Maison who was walking very carefully and then eased up. "We should be okay now," she said. I felt relieved too. I worried so much about her during all of this fighting. Just then the thought came to mind that Maison could come live with me in Overworld. She had done a good job of surviving the zombies. She and I could finish that tree house. We could go mining together, and I could show her the Nether. Not the Nether as a video game. The real Nether. She could build to her heart's content, making real houses, not little ones. She wouldn't have to wait until she was an adult to build a real house. Her dreams could start coming true now.

And I wouldn't have to try to make friends with the village kids. I wouldn't have to strain to impress them, because I already had Maison. I already had a friend. I couldn't stand the thought of losing her forever.

But I knew her coming to live with me in Overworld was a stupid idea. Her mom, her family, her whole world was here. I knew she complained about parts of it, but

I also knew that deep down inside she liked it here. She would never want to leave.

"We just need to check my room!" Maison exclaimed. "Then we can close the portal." But when we stepped into her room, we found the mob we'd missed during our search.

Standing right in front of the computer portal was a creeper. It looked at me with its frowning face and its black eyes, and when it saw us, it began to shake.

CHAPTER 18

THERE WAS NO TIME TO THINK. I HURLED MY SWORD with all my might. It flew through the air and struck through the creeper, making it vanish. I sagged with relief.

Maison gasped. "Stevie, that was so close!"

Boy, did I know it. I didn't realize until after I'd hit the creeper that I was shaking, and shaking hard. I'd taken one look into those black eyes and remembered the night at the tree house. The explosion. The pain. If I'd hesitated for even a moment, all of that would have happened again. It would have blown up Maison's house and maybe even killed her.

Then, I knew for sure I had to destroy the portal and I couldn't ask Maison to come live in the Overworld with me. As much as I wanted to think of another solution, I knew there was no other way around this situation. Never seeing Maison again wouldn't hurt as much as knowing I'd brought harm to her. No matter how I felt or how much my heart hurt, I would take apart the portal for her sake.

"Maison," I began, turning to her. Maison had dropped the fire poker and picked up her baseball bat from behind the bed. She gave the baseball bat a few test swings.

"There!" she said proudly. "I'm ready."

"What do you mean?" I asked.

"I'm going through the portal with you," she explained. "I'm going to help you get your dad."

I tried to say something but all words failed me. She still hadn't realized what it meant to close the portal.

"Maison . . ." I began again.

"Let's go," she said. "Before another creeper tries to get through!"

"Maison," I said. "Do you know what it takes to make sure we never let the mobs go through the portal again?"

"Yeah," she said easily. "So let's get going!"

She obviously didn't know. Maybe her *Minecraft* video game didn't work like my world, even though she said it was about my world.

I guessed maybe she could follow me into my world and we'd get Dad, and after Dad knew what was going on, I could tell her the truth about the portal. Then we would have to say our goodbyes and she would go back through the portal, back through her computer, into her world. Forever.

"All right," I said with an uncomfortable nod, gripping my sword. "Let's go."

We hesitantly moved toward the computer. I could see the Overworld through the screen. The problem was that the screen looked so solid. It wasn't swirling colors or looking like a normal portal. I put the tip of my sword to the screen. It sank through, without hurting the screen or changing the picture on the other side.

I glanced back at Maison, who was watching the sword closely.

"Remind me to never touch that computer screen unless I mean it," she said.

I took a deep breath. And then I plunged in.

It was awkward because I had to jump up to do it, but it worked. I saw the computer portal coming right at me, and then I was out of Maison's room and surrounded by colors. First there were the pulsing greens. Then everything turned a sky blue, and finally my whole world went red as a spider's eyes.

I plopped out at the other end, back in a world where everything looked so square and blocky and right. Home! As much as I'd enjoyed Maison's world, I had to admit that this was the world that just felt right in the end.

But there wasn't time to celebrate. Because almost immediately I noticed three things: the sky was overcast. My dad, a few feet away, was battling off a group of zombies. And the color red was shining right in front of me, but it had nothing to do with the portal. The red I was seeing was the eyes of a giant spider inches from my face.

CHAPTER 19

"**S**TEVIE!" DAD HOLLERED OVER THE ZOMBIES. INSTANTLY, I jabbed my sword out. It could have been a direct hit, but I missed it by the tiniest amount, and the spider clamped its mouth down. Before my eyes the sword was smashed to bits.

I dropped the handle and tried to grab the spider, using all my strength to push it back. It wasn't going to work. I wanted to call out to Dad, but I could see he was already trying to rush over to me, only to be blocked off by zombies. His diamond sword was flashing, trying to break through in time.

Right then a giant stick hit the spider over the head, knocking it back. The spider stumbled, shook itself, and looked again. Maison stood right over me, brandishing her baseball bat.

"Come and get me, you overgrown tarantula!" she shouted. "You don't attack my friend!"

"Maison!" I said in relief.

The spider charged, but Maison was too quick. She drew the baseball bat back over her shoulder before sending it swinging. It hit the spider straight in the face, flipping it back and making it disappear.

"Stevie!" Dad cried, his voice really panicked this time. I'd never heard him sound like that. He was still slashing his way through the zombies to get to me, but the spider's attack and Maison's appearance through the portal must have distracted him. He'd let his guard down for the slightest second and the mobs were all over him, circling him, pulling him down into the center of their swarm.

"Dad!"

I couldn't get to him in time. A zombie swiped at him just right, knocking the diamond sword from Dad's hand. The sword flew up in the air, sparkling against the gray sky before landing on the ground just out of Dad's reach. The blade knifed down into the ground while the handle trembled in the air from the force of the zombie's blow.

I dove for it, seizing the handle. Dad became lost inside the circle of zombies.

Was it already too late? Quickly I leapt toward the zombies, raising my weapon, desperate to break through the group and get Dad to safety.

I'd never actually held his diamond sword before. Now I swung it with all my might, drawing my arm back like Maison had done with her baseball bat. And Maison was beside me, attacking the zombies along with me.

One swift, sparkling swipe of the sword and some of the zombies fell, one by one.

The rest of the zombies turned from Dad to stare at Maison and me, but that was fine, I was ready. The diamond sword bit clear through the mobs. There were ten zombies, swarming all around me. My vision was full of flashes of blue as I flung out with the sword. The zombies kept getting right up close to me, their breath on my face, but each time they got that close I would hit back, slicing them with the sword before they could actually touch me. Ten zombies turned into five, and then two. And now I was facing the last one. It plunged toward me, only to disappear as soon as it touched the tip of the diamond sword's blade.

Now there was only Dad, Maison, me, and the portal. The mobs were gone.

CHAPTER 20

"**S**TEVIE," DAD SAID IN WONDER. HE WAS REALLY HURT, but he tried to sit up and couldn't. He sat back down and looked up at me in awe. "What happened? Where were you? I was so worried."

There were too many things he wanted to say and ask that all seemed to come out at the same time.

"I went through the portal," I said, pointing.

"And who is this?" He looked toward Maison.

"This is Maison," I said. "I met her at the other side."

Dad reached into his pouch where he kept food and milk. He needed these things now to regain his strength. There was an uncomfortable silence as all three of us stood there, still overwhelmed from adrenaline, trying to understand that we really were safe. For the moment, anyway. Some clouds began to break apart and let sunlight through. It felt different from the sun in Maison's world, but it was so good to have that light shine down and protect us from the dangerous mobs.

"If you're Stevie's dad, we need to get something straight," Maison said firmly. "You have no right telling him you're disappointed in him. Do you know what just happened? Stevie came out into my world, which I don't think anyone from the *Minecraft* world has ever done before. And when I took him to school with me, the mobs came out too and attacked. But do you know what? Stevie knew what to do and he saved everyone at the school. I'm talking about hundreds of kids."

I could tell Dad wasn't used to being talked to this way. He was The Steve, not someone you could lecture! But then he said, "You saved all those people?"

"He did," Maison said, crossing her arms.

"Well, Maison helped," I said, because it wasn't fair otherwise. "She acted like a general and told the kids what to do. She also followed me here and took care of that spider with a baseball bat."

"But you were the one who reacted when the zombies were first there," Maison said. "And you made all those weapons out of trees. Those kids needed something to protect themselves with, and no one else would have been able to make weapons that fast. And you had your sword."

We both looked down at my broken-to-bits sword from shop class. Nothing I made ever seemed to stay in one piece.

"You both saved all those children," Dad said. "And you saved me."

"And that's why you should never be disappointed in your son," Maison said.

Dad looked down. "I'm not. I shouldn't have said that. Stevie, is that why you ran away? I came home and looked everywhere for you. I could have kicked myself for what I'd said. It just came out, because . . . I didn't want to admit how scared I was of losing you."

I was stunned. Maison looked proud of herself for turning the conversation this way.

"What you did on the tree house wasn't the best way of handling things," Dad said. "You hadn't kept track of time and you panicked when you saw the creeper instead of fighting it. But we all make mistakes. I guess the point is to learn from them." He pushed more food into his mouth. I think it was partly because he really did need the food to heal up, but also partly because it was an excuse for him not to talk. I knew it was hard for my dad to say these things. He always liked to look so in-charge and never show his emotions.

But I needed this moment. After all the years of "Stevie, what were you thinking?" and "Stevie, you're doing that wrong," it was nice to have him finally say something positive. And know that he meant it. It was a start, at least.

I was surprised to hear Dad go on, "You were amazing with the diamond sword. I see I did train you well."

Maison gave him a disapproving look. Dad cleared his throat and corrected, "I see you are skilled with a sword. And it takes more than me training you for you to be able to do what you did."

Maison smiled approvingly.

"We should go back home, Stevie," Dad said. "I need to rest for a bit. But your friend is welcome to come along. She can have something to eat and meet Ossie. Maybe in my garden I have something that will help her feel better."

"Feel better?" Maison said blankly.

"I assume you have allergies," Dad said. "You're so soft and not squarish."

Maison made a face. I said, "No, Dad, that's how people look in her world. She doesn't have allergies."

"Oh," Dad said. He didn't apologize to Maison for his misunderstanding. He would still have to work on that. "Well, if you want to come along, you're more than welcome."

"Wait," Maison said. "We took care of the mobs in my world, so we're safe for now. But we need to do something about the portal so more mobs don't get through. Our world doesn't have any mobs, so people don't know how to handle them there."

I sucked in a breath. So it had finally come down to it. We couldn't take Maison back to eat because that would leave the portal unattended. Sure, the sun was coming out now, but if the sun got covered by clouds again, more mobs could make their way through. The portal needed to be destroyed as soon as possible.

"Maison," I said, but I was looking at the ground. This was so hard. What do you say to someone you just met, who understood you like no one else did, and who helped you save a school and your dad? "So long"? "Nice knowing you"? Nothing would be good enough.

"What?" Maison said. "If you have some tools, we can get started right now."

"Maison," I said sadly, "the only way to protect your world from the mobs is to destroy the portal." Now I forced myself to look up at her. "I'm so sorry, Maison. This has to be goodbye."

Maison was alarmed. "No!" she said. "No, don't even tell me that!"

"I'm sorry, Maison." Wow, I'd blown it. I hadn't made it sound nice at all. I'd maybe saved a school and my dad, but I didn't know how to save this conversation.

"I'm not going to never see you again!" she went on heatedly.

"The only way for that to happen is if one of us lives in the other's world," I said. "I couldn't ask you to live here forever. Your family is in your world. Your mom. Your home. And I can't leave here. Even with all its problems, I love it here."

CHAPTER 21

SHE STARED AT ME FOR A LONG MOMENT. "THERE IS another way," she declared.

"There is?" A bit of hope clutched at me.

"Yes," she said. "We'll build an obsidian house around the portal. Creepers can't blow up obsidian. We'll put iron doors on it so no mobs can enter, and we'll put torches near it so no mobs can spawn near here at night. We can even put all sorts of booby traps with arrows in dispensers and pressure plates in the house just to be extra safe. I'm not saying goodbye, Stevie. We're keeping this portal!"

I looked to Dad. "She's right," he said. "That would work. And I've got a lot of obsidian sitting in storage back home that you could use."

This time I knew exactly what to do. I ran over to Maison and hugged her. "Maison, you're brilliant!" I said. "We can still visit both worlds, and we don't have to lose each other! You've saved the day!"

Together Maison and I built the house around the portal in the Overworld so we could keep it safe. For

years Dad had let his supply of obsidian sit around, waiting to make a great project out of it, because obsidian is
really hard to get. For my tree house I'd made the point
of getting all my own supplies, but Dad understood how
much this portal mattered and how important it was we
protect it right away. Out came the obsidian blocks and
Maison and I got to work.

It was a simple house, but it was effective. First we just
put up the walls, roof, windows, and door. I was able to
work rapidly, and Maison knew exactly where everything
should go. I knew she would make a great architect one day.

We used sticks and coal to make torches. The only
thing left would be the booby traps, though they'd have
to wait for another day because of the amount of time
that was passing. This house should be just fine without
them, but Maison figured we'd use them just to be extra,
extra, *extra* careful. As we were finishing up, the sun was
setting.

"I need to go home," Maison said. "My mom is
probably worried. And who knows what they think at
the school!"

We arranged a time for her to try coming back, a few
days later. That would give me more of an opportunity
to fine-tune the house (and hopefully nothing would go
wrong) and take care of the booby traps. I watched as
Maison stepped through the portal, hoping she would
make it back okay, hoping she'd be able to return and our
plan would work.

Quickly Dad and I made our way back home before it got fully dark, with me propping him up since

he was still kind of weak. In my one hand I held his diamond sword.

Ossie was at the door and eager to greet us. I shut the heavy iron door behind us, helped Dad sit, put the diamond sword back on the wall and got some more food for us. I was starved and the food in Dad's pouch had only helped him a little.

"Stevie," he said. "There's something else you should know."

"What?" I asked, setting up the food. Too bad we didn't have any cereal. I needed to get more of that stuff from Maison's world.

"It's not as if I haven't made mistakes, either," he said. "When I was twelve and got the diamonds to make my sword, I almost got killed."

"You did?" I was so shocked I almost dropped my food.

"Yes," he said. "I got so completely caught up in finding those diamonds that I didn't notice some mobs sneak up behind me. Luckily I wasn't alone. My father, your grandfather, was also there, and he saw the mobs and saved me. If he hadn't been there, well, let's just not think about it."

"I didn't know that," I said.

"Well," he said. "After that I made my diamond sword and practiced really hard with it. I promised myself I'd never be in that situation again."

Ossie rubbed against me, purring, and I reached down to pet her. "So you didn't?" I asked.

"No," he said. "I did. A few times. The latest being today. I had searched everywhere for you, and when I found that portal, I wondered if you'd gone through it. I thought, *No, he couldn't have.* Then I began to hope you had, because then maybe you were just safe on the other side. I was going to go through the portal, but then I saw all the mobs surrounding it and going in. Something was attracting them to that portal."

He continued, "Then some of the zombies attacked me, and I saw you flying out of the portal. When that spider broke your sword and came at you, I thought I'd lose you. Your friend Maison showed up and saved you and I got so caught up in what I was seeing that I didn't finish fighting the zombies around me. You saw what happened."

"Yeah," I said softly.

He reached into his pouch and pulled out the broken pieces of my shop class sword. I hadn't realized he'd grabbed them.

"Oh, that," I said, embarrassed. "It's not very good."

"Yes, it is," he said. "You used this to defend the lives of others. I think we should hang it on the wall, next to the diamond sword."

"Even though it's in pieces?"

"Especially since it's in pieces. It shows you used it."

Within minutes my broken sword was on the wall. We stood back, admiring it.

"I also like that weapon your friend had with her," he said. "I should make myself one of those."

"The baseball bat?" I said. "It's not really a weapon. It's supposed to be for playing games."

"What a strange world," he said.

CHAPTER 22

"**N**EED MORE OAK BLOCKS OVER HERE!" MAISON CALLED.
"I'm on it!" I said. It was several days later and Maison had safely returned back into the Overworld. Together we had started anew on my tree house, making it even bigger and better than my original plans for it. Maison had a whole idea for a balcony and everything and I was watching it come together before our eyes.

While we worked, she filled me in on what had happened since I left her world.

"Well, no one could really figure it out," she said. "I haven't told anyone that my computer is also a portal. So it's a mystery to them how you and the mobs all got out there."

"Was everyone okay from the attack?" I asked.

"A few kids got hurt, but nothing that a trip to the school nurse couldn't fix," she said. "We were all really lucky. Ms. Reid said she's going to teach us how to make swords in shop class class, and she said you're welcome back any time. She said she's been experimenting with different ways to make swords, but she still can't figure out how you made them so quickly.

She said if you ever come back, you're going to have to teach her and the class."

I laughed a little. "Well, all right."

"The principal also said you're an honorary student," Maison said. "My mom got there after everything was over. She was pretty freaked out about the mess the house was in, but mostly she was just glad that I was safe."

I was stacking up blocks of wood for one of the walls while Maison straightened furniture in the middle of the room. This time she'd made a bed, and she'd used three planks of wood and some wool. You know, the nice, normal way to make a bed. With this bed I could spend the night out here in the tree house if I wanted to sometime.

"And you wouldn't believe what happened to Mitch and Dirk!" she said. "They realize we saved them, and now they practically kiss my feet every time they see me. It's all, 'Maison, we're so sorry! Maison, we were wrong!' I told them they have to help me make my little house again because it's their fault it got broken."

Maison paused from work for a minute to go out on the balcony and lean on the railing, staring out at the land around us. "This blocky world is going to take some getting used to, but I kind of like it," she said. "It's a good place to visit, especially since I can help build things on a large scale."

"Hey, Maison," I said, a little uncomfortable. "Do you think it might be okay for me to come visit you in your world again?" After all the havoc I'd brought last time, I didn't know if she'd want me to come back. Ms. Reid might have wanted me back, but Ms. Reid didn't know I'd accidentally brought mobs with me and caused all those problems. Maybe Maison only wanted to come visit me and she didn't want me to go back with her.

But she smiled over her shoulder at me. "Of course!" she said. "I still have to teach you how to play baseball. A baseball bat really shouldn't be used as a weapon—it's just that desperate times call for desperate measures, and I'd say a mob attack is pretty desperate."

That about made me sigh with relief. "I think we need a few more blocks over here," I said. "What do you think?"

"I think you're right," she said, coming over to my side. "And I think this tree house is going to be perfect."

ALSO AVAILABLE FROM SKY PONY PRESS

The Quest for the Diamond Sword

An Unofficial Gamer's Adventure, Book One

by Winter Morgan

Steve lives on a wheat farm and likes to spend his mornings in the village and trade his wheat for emeralds, armor, books, swords, and food. One morning, he finds that zombies have attacked the villagers. The zombies have also turned the village blacksmith into a zombie, leaving Steve without a place to get swords. To protect himself and the few villagers that remain, Steve goes on a quest to mine for forty diamonds, which are the most powerful mineral in the Overworld. He wants to craft these diamonds into a diamond sword to shield him and the villagers from the zombies.

Far from his home, with night about to set in, Steve fears for his life. Nighttime is when users are most vulnerable in Minecraft. As he looks for shelter in a temple, he meets a trio of treasure hunters, Max, Lucy, and Henry, who are trying to unearth the treasure under the temple. Steve tells them of his master plan to mine for the most powerful mineral in the Overworld—the diamond. The treasure hunters are eager to join him. Facing treacherous mining conditions, a thunderstorm, and attacks from hostile mobs, these four friends question if it's better to be a single player than a multiplayer as they try to watch out for each other and chase Steve's dream at the same time.

Will Steve find the diamonds? Will his friends help or hinder the search? Should he trust his new treasure hunter friends? And will Steve get back in time to save the villagers?

ALSO AVAILABLE FROM SKY PONY PRESS

The Mystery of the Griefer's Mark

An Unofficial Gamer's Adventure, Book Two

by Winter Morgan

Steve is back and ready for more adventures! But this time the excitement lands closer to home. While walking home from the village, Steve is surprised to hear a loud *BOOM!* When he arrives, he finds his wheat farm destroyed and a huge crater where the wheat once grew. And his diamond sword is missing! Steve believes it's the act of a griefer with a lot of TNT. Devastated, Steve wants to rebuild and find his sword, but with his wheat destroyed, he must call on old friends to help him.

All together again, Lucy, Max, and Henry tell harrowing stories of their treasure hunts and conquests, and Steve discusses his strategy for rebuilding. They all go to sleep, excited to begin their plans. But when they wake up, Henry is missing!

Who is the griefer terrorizing Steve and the villagers? And how will Steve find the resources to rebuild his prosperous farm? With suspicion circulating and no answers to be found, Steve finds himself wrongly suspected of these crimes—and so he must find his friend and discover who the mischievous griefer is before something even worse happens.

$7.99 paperback • ISBN 978-1-63220-726-5

The Endermen Invasion

An Unofficial Gamer's Adventure, Book Three

by Winter Morgan

Steve is invited to participate in an elite building competition on Mushroom Island. His friends—Max, Lucy, and Henry—are impressed and want to join their friend on a journey to the island. Steve asks his neighbor Kyra to come to the competition and help the gang build boats to get to Mushroom Island. She agrees, and the group sets out on an adventure to the contest.

After their exhilarating and rewarding journey to the contest, they finally make their way onto the island and meet the judges, as well as the other four contestants, whose egos are as big as the houses they are building. Steve builds his dream house to impress the judges, but in the middle of the competition, the island is overrun with Endermen. Mushroom Island is known for not having hostile mobs, so everyone knows it's the work of a griefer. Is it one of the contestants? Nobody knows, but they all have to work together to battle this invasion of the Endermen.

Will they be able to defeat the Endermen and find out who the griefer is? And who will win the building contest? Find out in this thrilling third installment of the Unofficial Gamer's Adventure series!

$7.99 paperback • ISBN 978-1-63450-088-3

ALSO AVAILABLE FROM SKY PONY PRESS

Treasure Hunters in Trouble

An Unofficial Gamer's Adventure, Book Four

by Winter Morgan

In this fourth installment of the Unofficial Gamer's Adventure series, Steve receives a distress call from his friends Max, Lucy, and Henry. They have found an abundance of treasure in a temple, but they can't get out! He immediately sets off for the desert to help his friends. Once Steve gets to them, they will all be rewarded with a supply of emeralds, gold ingots, and many other rare treasures.

But saving his friends and helping them extract the treasure isn't as easy as he thinks it will be. He enlists the aid of a neighbor to help him on his quest. With his friend Kyra in tow, the two brave a trip through the nether, get stuck at sea, face hostile chicken jockeys, and become trapped in a cave filled with spiders. They have to find their way to their treasure hunter friends while battling hostile mobs in this tale about trickery and treasuring friendship.

Will Steve be able to brave the Nether and rescue his friends? And will anyone get to go home with chests full of treasure? Find out in this thrilling fourth installment of the Unofficial Gamer's Adventure series!

$7.99 paperback • ISBN 978-1-63450-091-3

ALSO AVAILABLE FROM SKY PONY PRESS

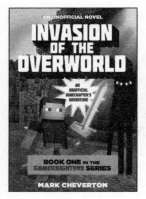

Invasion of the Overworld

Book One in the Gameknight999 Series: An Unofficial Minecrafter's Adventure

by Mark Cheverton

Gameknight999 loved Minecraft. He reveled in building structures, playing on servers, creating custom maps, and more. But above all else, he loved to grief—to intentionally ruin the gaming experience for other users. As the self-proclaimed "King of the Griefers," Gameknight played the game for himself at the expense of everyone else, keeping the list of his friends in the game short.

But when one of his father's inventions teleports him into the game, Gameknight is forced to live out a real-life adventure inside the digital world of Minecraft. What will happen if he's killed in the game? Will he respawn? Disconnect? Die in real life? Unsure, Gameknight must play the game with all of his skill and knowledge. He has to stay one step ahead of the sharp claws of zombies and pointed fangs of spiders. Eventually, he discovers the best-kept secret about Minecraft, something not even the game's programmers realize: the creatures within the game are alive!

This action-packed homage to the worldwide computer game phenomenon is a runaway publishing smash and the perfect companion for Minecraft fans of all ages.

$9.99 paperback • ISBN 978-1-63220-712-8

ALSO AVAILABLE FROM SKY PONY PRESS

Battle for the Nether

Book Two in the Gameknight999 Series: An Unofficial Minecrafter's Adventure

by Mark Cheverton

As *Invasion of the Overworld* ends, Gameknight999 and his friend Crafter find themselves on a new Minecraft server. Knowing the lives of all those within Minecraft—as well as those in the physical world—are depending on them, Gameknight and Crafter will need to search the land to recruit an NPC army if they are to stand a fighting chance.

Malacoda is the King of the Nether, a terrible ghast that has a vile, evil plan for the destruction of Minecraft. His massive army includes blazes, magma cubes, zombie pigmen, and wither skeletons, and his plans will take one of Gameknight's closest friends from him. Gameknight999 will have to sift through the chaos and put his Minecraft-playing skills to the test to solve the mysterious disappearance of all the crafters. But the battles Gameknight fought on the previous server and the enemy he faced have left him doubting his strength and his knowledge, and he'll need to reach deep inside himself to summon all the courage he has if he's to have any shot at victory.

Epic battles, terrible monsters, heartwarming friendships, and spine-tingling suspense . . . *Battle for the Nether* takes the adventures of Gameknight999 to the next level in a nonstop roller-coaster ride of adventure.

$9.99 paperback • ISBN 978-1-63220-712-8